Desire

Cypress Hill

Book #2

Told by

LaVeL Regine

Credits

Illustrations by

LaVeL Regine

Edited by

Renee Regine

CScottGroupInc.

2020

This Page Left Blank Intentionally

Scott Publishing House

A subsidiary of CScottGroupInc.

Copyright © 2019 LaVeL Regine

All rights reserved.

See more from author at:

www.lavel.uk

ISBN-13: 978-0-9854322-4-9

DEDICATION

I dedicate this body of work to the power of choices and the impact they have on lives.

CONTENTS

Chapter 1

Behind The Veil

I remember that day as if it just occurred. It started the same as all the ones prior it. Only that day did not end the same as the others had. Instead, it was the final blow to my already shattered confidence. The blow that would cause me to shut myself off from the world. The inevitable, as I have come to understand it.

Twenty-Seven years I lived hiding behind that veil. Frightened by the idea of someone catching a glimpse of my truth. The harsh reality that I found myself imprisoned to. It started at my right cheek and without regard stretched and coiled around my entire body. I was told it was a rare skin disorder. I was born with it for whatever reason. However, that never stopped the hazing growing up.

My father Ezekiel would often tell me that beauty was subjective. Though deep down I knew that a subjective view was not enough to blind a man. I recall as a young girl pondering finding true love. I believed it would take a blind man for me to do so. A man that could not see what a horror I truly was. Even that would not have been enough considering my skin was as rough as alligator hide. Therefore, my true love would have to be both blind and without the sense of touch. The chances of finding that man was not likely. So, I gave up on the foolish thought of finding true love.

For that, my life became a burden through and through. Not a burden that I carried alone. Instead, one that I shared with my father. He was my world up until he decided to take his own life last fall. I often blame myself for his suicide. He must have been ashamed. You know, having a daughter in my condition in all. He always assured me that was not the case. Still my mind would often beg the differ. I kept this to myself of course.

My father was my shield. He protected me from the harshness of the world. He also comforted me when that harshness sometimes got past the vail... When rude comments such as lizard girl or freak would leave me devastated buried beneath my pain and tears, he was there. He was the only thing that could bring me back in fact.

His love was like no other. It was all I expected from life. Truthfully, it was all I needed. It was more than enough. Hence why my life was shattered into pieces when he left me. I was left feeling as though I was without direction.

Surely, he would have told me to stay home that day. I would have listened to him as I always did. He had a keen sense of knowing what was best. I respected him for that. Despite at times his concerns were overstepping, I heeded the commands of his interests regarding my safety. I knew my best interest was at heart.

In his absence it was my care givers daughter Rachel that tried to fill his shoes. She was a good friend. One in which whom I had trusted and cared for dearly. Other than my father, she was the closest thing I had to family. We have been good friends' our entire lives. I was born one year before her but on the same day in fact. Both of us at Cypress Hill even.

My mother Olivia died when I was two years old. So, Rachel's mother Jennifer cared for me as if I were her own child. Rachel and I there after grew up as sisters. We both took a liking to one another instantaneously. We were inseparable.

"Two peas in a pod," as Mother Jennifer called us.

Mother Jennifer is what I was told to address Jennifer. Father Ezekiel said it was out of respect for my mother. The funny thing is Rachel and I both called her that. To us, she was our mother no matter what we called her. Same with father for that matter. Father Ezekiel was just the title we addressed him by. In our hearts, he was our father regardless. The four of us were one big happy family for quite a while. Twenty-five years to be exact.

When Father Ezekiel past, it was Rachel that gave me comfort and I her. Just as it was so when Mother Jennifer past two years earlier. I believe therefore by default Rachel became my new vail of protection. She was all I had left. She was my new world and I was hers. Two peas in a pod.

She was much different than Father. The two of them would often butt heads when it came to me and my wellbeing. She believed I needed to give the world a chance. While on the other hand he believed the world was no place for someone like me. Their last argument still rings vividly in my ears as I recall Rachel screaming at the top of her lungs,

"Father Ezekiel, sir with all due respect Desire is a young woman now and deserves to be treated as such!"

Father Ezekiel responded with a silent mumble underneath his breath, "well then see."

He shut himself away in his office for the last time that night. I found him the next morning dearly departed. I did not blame Rachel for his death, and she reassured me I was not to blame either. We both knew he had longed for it since Mother Jennifer had passed. The two of them were lover. That is why it did not take Rachel nor I by surprise when he confessed to being Rachels biological father in his suicide note. We both on some level already knew this to be the case.

We buried father next to our mothers in the family cemetery at Cypress Hill the following day. Our worlds were shattered. However, we held the glue that could mend the pieces back together, one another. It was Rachel that suggested it was time to leave Cypress Hill. She said that it was time I learned to be a woman and live life according.

In a way, I agreed with Rachel. I was a woman and was ready to experience what life was like as one. So, less than a month after father's passed Rachel and I moved from Cypress Hill. We decided to see what else the world had to offer. We ended up in London. Two open minded young women ready to take the world by storm. Or at least we would like to have believed so.

We chose London due to the stories father told us as a child. According to them it is there where he and my mother Olivia fell in love. He spoke of it as a forbidden love but one that he could not refuse nor deny. I believed that if a forbidden love could transpire between my parents in London. Then London was where my chance at love would be possible as well. Words cannot explain how I longed for that belief to be true.

The first few weeks in London I was more frightened than I had ever been in my entire life. Rachel worked tirelessly to pull me from my shell. Every so often she would talk me into going to a local coffee boutique for breakfast. I always wore my full head dress and veil. People just assumed I was Islamic following my culture. The only ones that knew the truth was Rachel and me. I found comfort in that.

Rachel always tried to talk me out of wearing them. She would say encouraging things like,

"You are so beautiful Desire; when will you allow the world to experience such beauty?"

Her kind words always made me feel good about myself. However, not good enough about myself to remove the vail. It was not until that day I felt good enough to remove the veil. The day everything in my life seemed to change in an instant. To my surprise, it was not Rachel's kind words that gave me the courage to do so. It was the kind words of a stranger. His voice was a delight that caught me by surprise.

Rachel and I had plans to meet at the coffee shop. Usually we would have gone together. However, she had plans of her own that day. Earlier that week she had fell into the likings of a handsome young Englishman. The two of them had grown quite found of one another. I contribute my own reckoning of truth to my sister's new acquaintance. I knew I had to get out more. I knew that if I were to find love, I would have to put myself out there to do so.

That day when I got to the coffee boutique Rachel had yet to arrive. I took a seat in the booth we always had and ordered my usual Chia Tea Latte and an English muffin with butter on the side. Nothing seemed out of the ordinary at first. I read the fashion articles in the daily paper as I always had. My order arrived at my table in just about three minutes exact as always and I briefly glanced from behind the paper to thank the waitress. It was then when the most peculiar thing occurred....

A man entered the boutique. Quite a frantic fella from what I observed. He appeared as if he was in a hurry. I passively watched the man from behind my paper as he made his way to the counter to place an order. His entire suggested that he was not a local. When he spoke, I pegged his accent as American?

He ordered a Chia Tea Latte and an English muffin with butter on the side. I must admit it took me by somewhat of a surprise. I was even more baffled when he began to make his way over to my booth. At first, I thought perhaps he was just headed in my direction and not necessarily to my booth. However, that notion proved to be wrong when he stopped at my booth and asked to join me.

"Excuse me, do you mind if I join you," the fella asked cunningly?

Briefly, I sat in silence and just stared at him. I could not believe he was asking to join me. My silence was interrupted by his proper introduction.

"How rude of me, Benjamin Whip is the name," he said as he extended his hand out to me for an introductory handshake.

I was hesitant to entertain his gesture. I am not quite sure why considering I was trying to put myself out there to find human companionship. It was not as if he was unattractive either. In fact, he was quite the opposite. He was very tall and handsome to say the least. He must have stood about six feet two inches or so. He had fair skin and dark curly hair that seemed to make his piercing blue eyes appear even more intense than they were. His voice was deep and smooth. I recall having a sense of soothing bestowed upon me as he attempted to catch my attention once more.

"Well Madam, if it is a bother, I shall be on my way then," Benjamin said as he nodded his head politely and turned to leave.

"Just a minute sir," I said as I reached out and touched his hand.

When he turned back to me, he was wearing a smile. I could see dimples in his cheeks and his teeth were vividly white. Benjamin was quite a handsome fellow. I knew from that moment he was the companion I sought.

"Please, join me if you would," I said as I stared up into his eyes.

He did not hesitate to take a seat or make himself comfortable. This seemed to come quite natural to him. Once seated he gestured to the waiter and had his food brought over to him. From then forward things fell into place all on their own.

"So, you know my name I think it would be nice if I knew yours as well," Benjamin suggested as he prepared his tea.

"Do excuse my rudeness, my name is Desire Vegas and it is a pleasure to make your acquaintance Benjamin," I said charmingly wearing an inviting smile underneath the vail.

"The pleasure is all mine Desire," Benjamin said while raising his brow accompanied by a one-sided smile. Desire, that is a fascinating name," he continued before taking a drink of his tea. "Do tell me Desire if you will, what is the meaning of your attire," Benjamin asked boldly confronting the elephant in the room?

Before my mind could process what was occurring, I responded,

"My attire, what do you mean Benjamin?"

"Well you know, the head dress and the veil around your face...," Benjamin explained in a humble tone.

I knew what Benjamin was asking. I just was not sure how to respond. I wanted to give him the truth, but I felt that if I did, he would get up and excuse himself from the table or even worse request to see my truth. I did not want either of those outcomes to occur, so I lied.

"It is a religious situation that I'd rather not get into at the moment Benjamin," I said while trying to hide the deception from my tone.

"I see, interesting," Benjamin replied just before smiling.

His smile could melt a woman's heart. I believe he knew this fact. Or at least that it was melting mine. I smiled back and gave a giggle knowing the gesture would suggest I was charmed by his presence. I was okay with that. In fact, I wanted him to know that I was interested in him. I believe that is why I asked him the next question. It took him by surprise and made him blush. It took me by surprise that he answered the question.

"So, before we get ahead of ourselves Benjamin what are your intentions with me," I asked as I boldly stared into his eyes?

There was a moment of silence that filled the booth briefly. But then in a stern and assuring voice Benjamin revealed his intentions. Those words rolled off his tongue majestically. They seemed to pierce my heart and soul and by the time he had said his final word I was smitten for him.

"To be quite honest Desire my intentions are to have you in every way possible. You see from the moment I laid eyes on you I have been allured to you. I am infatuated by you. Your presence resonates my soul. Though we have met just now I feel as if I have known you for eternity. I feel as if our souls are but one soul. As if our destinies are but one destiny. This is our fate Desire. Can you feel it," Benjamin proclaimed as I stared into his hypnotic eyes that seemed to peer into my soul?

I knew the words I wanted to say to him. They were on the tip of my tongue in fact. As I contemplated them in my mind his patients comforted me. It was as if he not only understood my silence, but he also respected it. I was not sure how, but I knew that over the duration of the small time we spent in that booth together I grew found of Benjamin... As I began to elaborate, I was interrupted by Rachel. She had finally arrived at the boutique to find Benjamin in her seat.

"Well Benjamin, I have to say," I was able to get out before Rachel made her presence aware.

"Well good morning Desire and who is this gentleman dinning with you," Rachel said as to announce her presence?

"Rachel... well good morning sister, this is Mr. Benjamin Whip, Benjamin my sister Rachel," I said in a flattering tone.

"Well then, Rachel it is a pleasure to make your acquaintance," Benjamin said as he stood to his feet.

"Benjamin," Rachel replied as she nodded her head to gesture the acquaintance.

"I best be taking off then leave you ladies to it I suppose," Benjamin suggested now wearing a disappointed smile. "My dear Desire perhaps we shall resume our discussion say tomorrow," he continued?

"Tomorrow," I asked?

"Yes tomorrow, of course if you are up to it," Benjamin replied followed by his heart-warming smile?

"Of course, tomorrow then," I said optimistically.

"Well then, it's a date," Benjamin replied. "I will meet you here tomorrow same time as today same booth preferably," he went on in a charming tone. Rachel, again it was a pleasure, he said before excusing himself from our presence. "You ladies enjoy the rest of your day now goodbye."

After Benjamin was gone a certain silence replaced him in the booth that morning. Rachel sat where he had and just admired me. She did not say one word, she just smiled.

Chapter 2

Truth Be Told

Later that evening as I expected Rachel could no longer fight her urge to ask. I was sort of relieved that she did because by then I was dying to tell her. We were in the sitting room listening to classical music while enjoying an evening fire. I was having my night cap, a glass of Chateau Margaux 1875 while watching her paint as I did most nights. I found her intensity and passion quite soothing. Subtlety, without breaking her focus from painting she asked in a manner as to not pry.

"So, that was an interesting gentleman today at brunch," Rachel suggested without skipping a stroke of her paint brush. "A handsome fellow too," She went on.

"Yes, he was quite the character," I said trying to be modest. "I really enjoyed his company today and look forward to seeing him tomorrow," I continued.

"Is that so," Rachel asked? "He must have made some impression," She went on?

The room filled with a brief silence due to my lack of response. I had found myself drifting away in the idea of seeing Benjamin again. I could smell the scent of his cologne as if he were in the room. I felt warm at the idea of staring off into his eyes again. The vibration of his voice capturing my soul. His gentle touch against my skin. His strategic pursuit to win my heart. I did not realize how deep I had succumbed to my thoughts until they were interrupted by Rachel.

"Are you fond of him," Rachel asked?

"Well to be honest I believe so, very much in fact," I explained. "It was something about his presence that resonated with me. I felt as if I knew him though I had only just met him. I could have lived in that moment with him there in that booth for eternity and I strongly believe he feels the same," I went on without holding back...

A part of me was waiting on Rachel to give the approval of my new-found infatuation for Benjamin. After all it was her who suggested I should lead a normal life, love included. Instead, she caught me by surprise with her conservative advice.

"Well, let's not get a head of ourselves now Desire you only just met the fellow," Rachel suggested. "Give it some time and see how things go before you surrender your heart and soul," she continued. "I am assuming you didn't tell him; I mean... you know," Rachel said as to catch herself trying not to offend me.

Though I knew she had my best interest at heart, I had every intention to disregard her advice. I knew what I felt. More importantly, I knew that what I felt was real. I lived my entire life thus far behind the veil. The garment that covered my face as well as the safety net that protected me from the outside world. Truth be told, I had enough of the veil.

I was ready to see what a normal life could be like. Although I was not sure how to explain that to Rachel, I wanted to. However, I did not want to upset her. Nor was I prepared to lose her. I was afraid that if I did not take her advice it would result in both. So, I told her what she wanted to hear.

"You are right Rachel," I replied agreeingly. "I will take things slowly with Benjamin," I continued. "After all, I barley even know the guy," I went on before taking the last drink of my glass of wine.

"Good, that sounds safe Desire," Rachel insisted. "I just don't want you to get hurt, you know," She continued?

"I understand Rachel," I replied as I stood to my feet and walked over to her. "I know you are trying to protect me, and I appreciate that, thank you," I continued as I preceded to give her a hug.

She stopped painting only long enough to reciprocate my affection. Then as if there were never an interruption, she became one with the painting once again.

"Well I am going to retire for the evening Rachel, do enjoy the rest of your night," I said as I left the room.

"Good night Desire. I will see you in the morning beautiful," Rachel replied.

As I laid in bed that night, I realized that Rachel had took father's place in more ways than she knew. She had now become my protector instead of my encourager. At least it seemed that way in regard to love. I had the notion to tell her of this but decided against it. I believe because a part of me missed father's protection. Knowing Rachel now possessed it made me feel safe.

That night I had a dream of Benjamin. It was a rather peculiar dream. The two of us ... to say the least we were lovers. It appeared as if we had been for some time. The way he looked upon me and I him was as if nothing else in the world mattered. The dream started pleasant. We were on a canoe traveling down a calm river on a beautiful spring day. He stood at one end paddling wearing a smile of content that suggested there were no other place he would rather be. I sat at the other admiring him admire me.

The birds chirped majestically. The wind blew suddenly in such a fashion that it felt like silk across my skin. There were but a few clouds in the sky and the sun pierced from between them as if they gave birth to it. The subtle movement of the river gave off a tranquil sound. I found myself caught in a hypnotic trans caused by the combination of the attributes of that day. It truly was a blissful day. I hoped it would never end.

Then without notice it began to shower. It started as just a mild midst and felt rather refreshing. The mist intensified as storm clouds swiftly seized the sky. The sun seemed to dissipate before my eyes in a way that suggested it was taking cover from the storm to come. The gentle winds became ferocious and the rivers water rapid. Lighting illuminated the newly darkened sky and thunder roared as if it meant to make its presence aware

Through this intense transformation Benjamin remained calm as if nothing had changed. He stood at the front of the canoe still wearing his smile of admiration steadily paddling our way. I had grown concerned because the canoe had begun to shake caused by the mighty wind. It had also begun to be filled by the rain fall. Behind me I could hear a mighty clashing of water, so I turned to investigate. What I saw invoked terror in me that is hard to describe. A terror that haunts me even during waking hours.

Only a few meters away was a waterfall that had appeared out of know where. We were headed directly towards it. I tried to call out to Benjamin but know sound came out of my mouth. It was as if my voice had been frightened away. I tried to stand to my feet, but I could not move a single muscle. I was in a sense paralyzed staring down an inevitable fate, demise.

I wrestled with the intent to move and speak only briefly. For as we grew closer to the fall in a strange way, I embraced its beauty. In the midst of my terror and the extreme conditions surrounding peace was everywhere. As the small canoe began to make its way over the fall, I took a deep breath and embraced whatever was to come. To my surprise, instead of falling the canoe flew.

It was then when my mysterious paralyses subsided, and my voice returned all at once. I anxiously stood to my feet and turned to Benjamin and there he was still standing in the position as he had from the start. I softly called his name, but he did not hear it.

"Benjamin," I called out to find my voice had returned.

He did not respond, nor did I expect him to. Instead, steadily he paddled our way now through the clouds as they parted and made way for our sake. He was still wearing that smile that I adored and that look on his face that always seems to melt my heart. In that moment, I knew that there was something magical about Benjamin and I aimed to make its accord.

I stood breath taken and speechless and admired him as he did I. The two of us soaring through the sky without a care in the world. I thought to make my way over to him. To give him a great big hug and a kiss. Perhaps profess my love to him as well. All of that would have been just fine and reciprocated I am sure. Despite that notion I decided to sit back down as I were before.

The storm had passed just as fast as it had come. The sun now more vivid than I had ever seen shined down on us. The birds flew alongside our mystical vessel just as amazed as I were by the whole ordeal, so it seemed. They sang magical song and as they did, I could see the musical notes come from their mouths. Soon the entire sky was filled with these notes.

I reached up and grabbed one and it burst in my hand like a bubble very similar to the ones I played with as a child. When the note burst a rainbow emerged from it and sprawled out in every direction. The rainbow possessed a vibration that filled me. I was consumed by its vibration in such a way that I felt myself begin to lose consciousness. As I drifted away into a harmonic bliss, I caught one final glimpse of Benjamin. He smiled, and I smiled back.

The following morning, I woke up more than eager to meet with Benjamin. I knew it had much to do with my dream. It may sound bizarre, but I felt as if somehow, He had visited me in that dream. I held the impression that there was something magical about him. After all, he had caused me to be smitten both in real-time and now even my dreams.

I had now grown quite found of him rather rapidly. Even Rachel warned against it. However, even she would agree that if ever there were a man who could win my heart it would be a man that could do so in both the wake and dream world. For me, that man was Benjamin. I wanted to tell Rachel but after our talk last night I decided to keep things to myself for a while.

Luckily, Rachel was still asleep after I had finished preparing for my date with Benjamin. I was able to slip out unnoticed. I was very eager to meet with him, so I was not surprised that when I made it to the boutique a little early, he had yet to arrive. However, I was a bit taken when I went to open the door and His hand beat mine to it.

"Allow me my lady," He said as he pulled the door open for me.

"Oh my, well thank you Benjamin," I said in a startled but pleased tone.

I was confused by his presence considering it almost seemed as if he just appeared out of nowhere. I mean it was impeccable timing on his part. I recall as we made our way to the cash register to place our order thinking amongst myself just how peculiar it was. I contributed it to his already mysterious nature. I looked forward to exploring deeper into that nature.

He took charge and order for the two of us. I was flattered by the gesture. I admired how handsome he looked while he placed our order. He had a sort of masculine elegance about him. His presence seemed to capture the rooms attention effortlessly. I used to be insecure of the type of attention he commanded but with him by my side it was not so bad.

After our order was placed, we made our way to a booth. I was pleased to find my usual one available. As a gentleman should, Benjamin helped me to my seat before taking his across from me. I had many questions that I wanted to ask him, so I wasted no time and dove right in with my first question.

"So, Benjamin do tell me what brings you all the way to London," I asked as he got settled into his seat and caught eyes with me.

"Well, would you like the long or the short version," He asked as the waiter made his presence to our booth to deliver our breakfast and tea.

Benjamin smiled at me as if he were pleased with his answer before turning and acknowledging the waiter. The gesture allowed me to contemplate on which version would be best suited.

"Thank you so much kind sir," Benjamin called out to the waiter as he served us.

Benjamin's voice pulled me from my momentary contemplation and back to his attention. His politeness was genuine. Observing it allowed me to comprehend why his presence was so captivating. I found myself caught in a trance of admiration. A nostalgic daydream of some sort.

"Well, long or short beautiful," Benjamin asked as he prepared his tea?

"Oh, do pardon me, the long version if you will," I suggested optimistically.

"I was hoping you said that because the short version just doesn't do the story justice," He suggested wearing a pleased smile.

I could tell from the look on his face I would be glad I requested the long version. Benjamin cleared his throat and took a big gulp of his tea before starting his story.

"Well you see, my story starts here in London," He said as he stared right down into my eyes. "It began quite similar to our story, so I was told," He went on before I modestly interrupted.

"Our story you say, how so," I asked in a curious tone?

"Well, my mother, Bernadette Harbor was only fourteen at the time. She was here in London with her folks. They were on Vacation celebrating her coming of age. My mother was a free-spirited young woman. More so, she was eager to get out and meet folks. And when I say folks I mean of the opposite sex. Bless her heart. She was determined and by any means necessary. Of course, that meant going against her family's strict courtship rules that suggested young women should be chaperoned in the company of young men. You see, my mother had a mind full of ideas of her own. A beautiful mind at times. Then other times, mischievous," Benjamin explained as I chimed in an interruption.

"Sounds familiar, however aren't all young ladies a bit curious and mischievous when it comes to getting their way Benjamin," I asked flirtatiously?

He let off a brief chuckle before continuing.

"I suppose," He said still wearing a smile. "Shall I continue," He went on to ask?

"Well, of course and please pardon my outburst Benjamin. At times I just cannot help myself. I contribute it to be a natural quality of a young lady I suppose," I said in a humorous tone.

The two of us shared a laugh before He continued his story.

"The night before my mother and her family were to leave London home bound my mother decided to sneak out," Benjamin said his voice once again filling our booth.

He paused there briefly to take a sip of his tea and I assumed anticipating me to interrupt him once again. Despite wanting to I fought the urge and restrained myself from doing so. He then smiled at me delightfully before diving back into his story.

"The funny thing about my mother sneaking out that night was the fact that they were on the second floor of the Brown's Hotel," Benjamin explained as he began to laugh. "You see my mother thought it would be a good idea to go out of the bathroom window and scale her way down using the sheets from her bed tied together as a rope," he went on. "Unfortunately, she did not really think this plan through, Benjamin explained fighting back his urge to laugh. "You see, my mother was in such a panic to make it out undetected she failed to realize the sheet rope she had constructed didn't quite reach the ground level. Instead, it left her dangling on the side of the building somewhere in between the second and first floors,"

Benjamin made out before bursting out into a hysterical laugh.

His laugh was contagious. I found myself unconsciously laughing along with him despite a part of me felt that it may have been inappropriate. A side from my laughter, I could not resist interjecting any more. I believe it was the thought of his poor mother dangling on the side of that hotel. I have to admit it was rather humorous, however I was concerned with her wellbeing. I had to know how on earth did she get down off the side of that Hotel. I interrupted our laugh with an anxious encouragement for Benjamin to continue his story. He was more than happy to oblige. It took him a moment to regain his composure. Once he did, he cleared his throat once more took a big gulp of his tea and continued.

"My poor mother," He said. "As she dangled there on the side of that hotel in fear of both her life and waking her parents she refused to call out for help," Benjamin continued.

"My Lord, she didn't call out for help, well what on earth did she do," I asked out of impulse?

"Well, like I said she didn't want to wake her folks and she knew that if she called out for help, they'd surely come running to her aid ending her extravaganza before it ever began," He explained. So, instead she waited there until a passerby saw her dangling and came to her aid," Benjamin continued.

"A passerby, well how long did she dangle there waiting on a passerby," I asked?

"Well, she dangled there for twenty minutes or so before an English man by the name of Jethro walked pass and saw her," Benjamin explained.

"Twenty minutes, that must have felt like an eternity," I interjected.

Benjamin let out a snicker before continuing.

"Jethro scaled the Hotel wall, took my mother onto his back and then scaled them both back down," Benjamin explained. "Luckily for me, the two of them fell in love and were inseparable after that," He went on.

He smiled and paused briefly before continuing.

"I was conceived out of that union," He said still wearing his smile. "Unfortunately, the union was short lived and ended when my mother returned home," He explained.

"Short lived, but what about the baby," I asked in a concerned tone?

"Neither of them knew my mother was pregnant, Benjamin said. "And they both knew that there was no way to sustain their relationship considering they were from two different parts of the world," He went on.

"Oh, I'm sorry to hear that Benjamin," I said compassionately to comfort him as I reached over and placed my hand on his.

Benjamin looked down at my hand then back up into my eyes and smiled before speaking.

"Well, there is no need in being sorry," He suggested. Everything happens for a reason... or something like that right, He suggested optimistically?

"I suppose so.... Surely, I do indeed hope so," I concurred.

Benjamin smiled at me before continuing. Then he paused briefly, and his eyes grew saddened.

"I only wish I would have had a chance to meet him," Benjamin proclaimed in a heartfelt tone. "Now, I am here in London settling a man's final affairs that I never met," He went on. "It feels a bit strange, but I know it's the right thing to do," he said before taking the final sip of his tea.

I felt Benjamin's pain. However, I was at a loss for words. I had recently lost my father and felt a similar pain. Though I felt Benjamins pain was much different. He had lost someone he never knew. Someone close to him but never truly close. Now he was left torn with the idea that he would now somehow subliminally meet his father while still never truly meeting him. The booth filled with silence. The silence was prominent yet not awkward. Instead, it was meaningfully peaceful.

The silence must have lasted for twenty minutes or more before it was broken. By this time, the two of us were done with our breakfast. I could not believe how fast time had went by. I felt like we had just sat down to dine but in actuality we had been talking for quite a while and then silent for just as long. I was not ready for our date to end so I was more than pleased when Benjamin asked me to take a morning stroll with him. Like a gentleman he stood to his feet look to me and reached down for my hand.

"Shall we beautiful," He asked charmingly as he took my hand and helped me to my feet?

He then proceeded to lead the way with his arm wrapped snuggly around my waist. I must admit I was rather flattered by his actions. He made me feel wanted. I was not sure where exactly we were headed next but to be honest it really didn't matter. As long as I was with that charming man, he could have led me anywhere and I would have gladly followed.

Chapter 3

A Walk Through The Park

Benjamin took me to Regent's Park in central London. He told me he was advised by a local to check the park out. He said the local told him that Regent's Park was one of the Royal Parks of London. He explained that the park was established in 1811 and was once part of a great chase, appropriated by Henry VIII. He explained these interesting facts about the park while wearing a big smile of enthusiasm. I admired Benjamin's passion for the park. It was refreshing.

The park was grand. It stretched out majestically over 410 acers of sheer bliss. It consisted of large open spaces with tree-lined pathways, formal gardens, enchanting ponds, and a plethora of diverse culture. Our first stop was Queen Mary's garden. The sight of the garden literally took my breath away. I believe its presence was heightened by its smell in which pleasantly greeted me as we approached it. The smell reminded me of Cypress Hill during the months of Spring. The smell of many varieties of roses simultaneously stimulating the sensory cortex.

While holding Benjamin's hand I brought our walk to a halt as we entered Queen Mary's Garden. I closed my eyes and took a deep breath of the rose infused air and in that moment, I could see myself as a young girl playing in the roses garden back home at Cypress Hill. I could see Rachel running through the maze plotted rows of roses calling out for a chase.

"Come on Desire, come play with me," Rachel would call out antagonizing a pursuit.

I could see Jennifer, our beloved mother bringing out chocolate chip cookies and lemonade for the two of us. A daily ritual it had become since as far back as I can remember. My father, Ezekiel just north in a small distanced visiting my biological mother Olivia's grave. The peace that was bestowed upon me within that moment was paralyzing. I must have stood there in that gracious archway of perpetual beauty present, yet not so.

When I finally opened my eyes, his beautiful smile welcomed me. His lips where slightly puckered and accompanied a dumbfounded look upon his face. I smiled with conviction with my eyes. I did so with enough attentive passion I imagined that I surely was stealing his heart right from his chest. The words that came out of his mouth confirmed.

"My lord... you are so beautiful," Benjamin said as he took his hands and placed them on my cheeks.

His hands had a slight chill and I could almost feel them through my head dress. His words made me smile. I knew he could feel it because I felt my cheek rise underneath his palms. His words touched me because I knew that when he called me beautiful, he was addressing me as a person and not just a pretty face. In fact, he had yet to see my face. The terror that lied beneath the veil. Although deep down I knew that reality still existed, Benjamin had a way about himself that made me forget.

With his hands now holding the back of my neck he pulled me in for a kiss. I admit his spontaneity caught me by surprise. However, his kiss was long awaited. Despite the garment that separated our flesh I could feel his lips were as I expected, soft and alluring. His eyes were closed as I saw when I opened mine momentarily to witness myself kiss that gorgeous man for the first time. I felt as if nothing could detour me from that magical moment.

Our kiss only lasted for what felt like seconds and I instantly longed for more. The kiss was modest but quite passionate. We did not exchange tongues as Rachel had once advised a good kiss involved. Despite that I acknowledged that kiss as the best kiss I ever had in my entire lifetime. Of course, it was my first kiss in which Rachel would insist must be considered.

As Benjamin slowly pulled from the kiss, we caught eyes. We lingered in that moment. I anxiously waited for him to engage further in what felt like an eternity. As he began to pull me back in for more our passion was abruptly interrupted. From what seem as if out of nowhere, a Basset Hound ran right into Benjamin. It almost knocked him off his feet. Luckily, he was able to agilely recapture his balance.

Rather than being upset by the shenanigans Benjamin appeared pleased. His sleek balance and composed nature were alluring. I found myself displaying a smitten demeanor. His big smile accompanied by a subtle chuckle defused the moment. As he reached down to aid the pup whose leash was now tangle around his legs an elder man approached.

"Oh, I am so sorry," the man called out as he reached down and help untangle Benjamin and the pup.

"No worries Sir," Benjamin replied.

Once the pup was free the man properly introduced himself and his pup.

"My name is Maxwell Titus and this young fella here is Rocky," the man explained. "Rocky here is a rescue and just a tab bit ill-mannered yet," Maxwell went on as he extended his hand out to shake Benjamin's.

Benjamin un-hesitantly reciprocated.

"My name is Benjamin Whip, and this is the beautiful Desire Vegas the pleasure is surely ours, Benjamin said.

"Well, again I am sorry little Rocky here ran into you," Maxwell reiterated.

"Oh, don't worried about it," Benjamin insisted as he reached down and began to play with Rocky.

"Well, I guess Rocky and I will leave you two to your day," Maxwell said.

Benjamin arose to his feet and shook Maxwell hand once more before him and Rocky went on their leave.

At the time I did not think anything of the brief encounter. It was simply a quirky event that took place that somehow seemed to make me fall even harder for Benjamin. As the two of us made our way through the spectacular garden we talked about everything. How he grew up believing his grandparents were his parents and his mother was his sister. His childhood dog Trixie who was a basset hound. He told me how bumping into Rocky reminded him of her.

He spoke of tradition rich holiday filled with family, cheer, and bliss. His favorite food which of all things was Crab Legs. I smiled at the idea considering that was my favorite cuisine as well. He mentioned how at fourteen being sent to Boarding School left him with resentment towards his family. How he never gave up on meeting his dream girl in which whom I resembled physically, mentally, and spiritually. Benjamin really open up to me that morning and I adored him for it.

To reciprocate I explained to him how my adolescent life was very much similar to his. How being sheltered in such a fashion that it made me feel as if I were being hidden left me with some resentment. How I too had a childhood dog whose named was Lilly. Lilly was a German Shepard and was just as pampered and sheltered as me. I shared with him how aside from moving to London I had never been outside of Cypress Hill's walls. How on a cosmic level I felt as if he was the reason why I did leave Cypress Hill? After all it was in fact to find true love.

Our conversation were effortless. The topics rose and fell like the steady flow of the tide. We both seemed to forget about time. It was as if time did not exist. It was not until I saw a boat that our attention from one another was disrupted. The boat reminded me of my dream and the day was turning out to be just as nostalgic. We both looked at one another and knew the others thought.

Benjamin smiled before taking my hand and asking, "Shall we?"

I nodded my head to oblige as he began to lead the way. As we walked towards the canoe, I found myself reminiscing about my dream. I felt the urge to tell Benjamin but kept it to myself. Mostly so because I was enchanted.

Enchanted by the idea of us. More so by the idea that Benjamin felt the same.

After renting the canoe Benjamin assisted me to board the vessel. He then boarded and sent the canoe into motion by giving the dock a stiff nudge with the paddle. Like in my dream he stood across from me at the front of the canoe gently fueling our motion with his focused effort while I gazed up at him in awe. Still lingering in my mind was that dream in which the day as it progressed more and more resembled.

I could hold it in no more. The urge to confess my dream had won over. As I tried to push the words out of my mouth Benjamin's voice cut me off.

"You know I had a dream of you last night Desire," He said as he turned and took a seat across from me.

His words caught me by surprise. They also aroused my curiosity. So, I decided to listen rather than sharing.

"A dream of me," I asked in an inquiring tone?

"Yes, a dream of you," Benjamin assured as he reached over for my hands. "Of course, I was in the dream and we experienced something that I can't stop thinking about," He went on before pausing....

"Well, go one do tell," I now insisted now even more curious of what occurred that was so unforgettable between the two of us in his dream.

"Well, it gets passionate and I don't want to offend, nor have you take it the wrong way," Benjamin explained.

"Oh, Benjamin we are both adults I assure you will not offend me, nor will I take what you say out of context," I suggested in an assuring tone. "Now, go on please continue," I went on to insist.

"Well.... We were happy, full of laughter and cheer," Benjamin explained wearing a pleased smile.

"Sounds nice," I chimed in eagerly before a brief silence.

"There is more," Benjamin went on eliminating the silence.

"Oh, there is," I asked hoping to keep him talking?

"Yes, There is....,"

"Well, are you going to tell me or leave me in suspense," I asked prior his smile causing me to blush.

Benjamin's voice once more eradicates giving birth to a brief silence, "In the midst of my laugh I looked up and caught a glimpse of you.... In that moment I could feel you, mentally, physically, and cosmically," he explained passionately.

Again, the canoe filled with silence. My attention was completely captivated. My interested undoubtedly aroused. My heart, smitten. Eagerly I coerced the continuance of his story.

"After you felt our connection," I asked?

"You caught a glimpse of me and felt the same," Benjamin explained.... In that moment, I knew you felt the same because it was as if I were you and you I, He continued. As if... we were one in the same...," Benjamin explained before I chimed in interrupting him.

"Opposite side of the same coin perhaps," I suggested.

"Perhaps," Benjamin concurred.... "I could hear your heartbeat as if it were my own. I could feel your desire for me. I could see your thoughts. They were filled with love, compassion, admiration, and lust," He went on.

I cleared my throat before speaking.

"Well I have to say that is some dream," I made out before Benjamin interjected.

"There's more," he insisted bring my response to an abrupt halt.

"There is," I asked now becoming slightly aroused by the idea of more?

"Yes, there is," Benjamin assured.... "You stood and came over to me. As I sat in a chair in front of the fireplace you went to your knees before me and stared up into my eyes. As I stared down into your eyes you ran your hands up my thighs. Up my stomach, my chest, my shoulders then around my neck before stopping there. You then gently pulled me into you. I un-hesitantly surrendered to the gesture. I leaned in and kissed your neck. Then your right cheek. Then your lips," Benjamin explained.

"Oh wow, I am at a loss for words," I suggested as I tried to maintain my composure.

Benjamin story was very arousing to say the least. It also made me feel even more comfortable with him. The fact that he was able to share something so intimate with me. The canoe filled with silence as we both regrouped. He smiled at me and I him as we gazed into one another's soul. I could feel his intentions as he leaned in for a kiss.

His hands ran across my cheek as his lips grew closer to mine. Time seemed to halt, and my heart raced. I could feel that which I had feared about to occur as Benjamin attempted to remove my headdress from covering my lips. I did not know what to do so naturally I panicked.

"Benjamin, wait," I suggested as I frantically stood to my feet causing the cane to rock sending Benjamin into the pond with a big splash disrupting a flock of geese.

"Oh, my lord I am horribly sorry Benjamin," I proclaimed as he came up from his sudden plunge.

I grabbed the canoe paddle and reached it out to him to assist him back on to the canoe. He took hold of my quick-witted lifeline and re-boarded the vessel.

"Well, I wasn't expecting that he suggested before bursting into a full out laugh.

His laugh caused me to as well. However, while I did feel bad that I had accidentally knocked him off the canoe; he did not seem to care. Instead he apologized.

"I'm sorry beautiful I didn't mean to startle you," Benjamin said charmingly. "I guess we better be getting me some fresh clothes then," He went on chipperly.

Our date ended early that day but lingered on throughout. One thing in particular that I found myself holding on to was Benjamin's invitation he extended to me before we parted ways. He asked if I would accompany him to his fathers will reading as support. I was more than eager to accept.

Chapter 4

Magical Mystical Land

That evening when I got home Rachel was there waiting for me. She seemed a bit agitated but did not speak. Instead, she gave me a look of disappointment. I knew I had to try and make things right. So, I told her all about my date with Benjamin. To my surprise, she was very much so pleased to hear that the date went well. In fact, in a way I believe she was now rooting for Benjamin and me.

I told her about his invite to his will reading. To my surprise, she thought it was a great idea that I accompany him. I was both glad and relieved that I had my sisters support in my new love venture. It really meant a lot to me. More than eager to see Benjamin again after our talk I went straight to bed.

That night I had the most amazing dream. I found myself submerged in some sort of a white light. The light was so bright all I could see was it. It was so intense that it stripped me of every thought I ever had. I found great pleasure in the peacefulness of the absence of thought. My mind willingly surrendered and went completely void. It was as if the only thing that existed was my awareness.

I was aware that I existed even though I could no longer see nor feel my physical body. I felt as if I had become the light. It bestowed upon me a sense of stillness. I was overtaken by a feeling of unification. A oneness with everything. A tranquil peace I had never felt before.

The dream was very lucid and captivating. I could not distinguish it between dream or reality. I found myself hoping it was reality. Honestly, I never wanted to leave that blissful moment. It was the first time I had ever truly felt carefree.

As I grew completely comfortable in the void of the light, I could feel my awareness being pulled from it. With all my might and intention, I tried to fight to remain submerged in its bliss. I knew that what I had experienced was a true gift. A gift experienced most likely only once in a lifetime. I believe it was that in which caused me to try and remain there. However, just as I found myself there in an instant I was gone.

I now found myself standing in a field of tall grass. The pastures stretched on in every direction farther than my eyes could see. The Sun shined down vividly and there was not a cloud in sight. I could feel the Sun warm presence which called my attention to it. As I briefly gazed up at it to show respect a pleasant breeze gave my skill a cool chill.

I closed my eyes face aimed up at the Sun and open my arms wide inviting its warm embrace. I took a deep breath and as I exhaled, I felt someone embrace me. I was not startled by the embrace. Instead, it made me become emotional. I believe because the embrace felt familiar. It reminded me of my father. Perhaps because the embrace was infused with his sent.

In that moment, my eyes still shut tightly I wrapped my arms around my embracer as if it was my father. I laid my head in his chest and wept. My embracer gently ran his hands through my hair as my father often would to comfort me. Then the most remarkable thing occurred. My embracer spoke.

"There... there Tulip... Everything is going to be just fine," the voice called out in a familiar tone.

His words grabbed my attention. Tulip is what my father called me. Often when I would cry myself to sleep, he would be there caressing my hair saying those exact words. I thought to myself could it be. At first, I was afraid to open my eyes and verify whether it was or not. However, I knew I had to.

I slowly opened my eyes and lifted my head from my embracer chest. When I looked up to him, I was greeted by my father's warm smile. I quickly threw myself back into his arms. I could not believe my eyes. How was it possible? Honestly, it did not really matter.

All that did matter was that I was wrapped firmly in my father's' arms. I was completely captured in a moment that I never wanted to end. It is funny how when you want something so bad most times you get the opposite. Perhaps due to the fear of the loss of that which you desire. Whatever the case, before I could tell my father how much I had missed him, he was gone.

I had woken up to my true reality. I looked over at the clock and it was 3:33 A. M. precisely. Only a few hours had passed since I had rushed off to bed. I tried aimlessly to fall back to sleep with hopes for just one more minute with my beloved father. I believe it was my desperation that made returning to sleep impossible. So, instead of sleep I just laid there staring at the ceiling. Full of sorrowful tears yet not one fell.

It was there lying in my bed that night when I realized what I was searching for. It was not simply love or even true love for that matter. It was deeper than that. Perhaps even on a metaphysical level. I am not sure; however, one thing was certain I was ready to find it.

I was not sure if Benjamin was exactly it. I was certain however that he sure did feel like it. It was the thought of him that finally ended my restlessness. Somehow from a far he was able to bring me comfort. So rather than crying my eyes out until daylight. I laid there comfortably wearing a smile of optimism.

Before I knew it, I heard the birds chirping outside my window. I was excited to hear the birds chirping. Not solely because they are out right beautiful to wake up to. More so, I was excited that shortly I would be meeting Benjamin. I could hardly wait to get our day started together.

I had thoughts of telling Rachel about my dream but decided to keep it to myself. I did not want to put a damper on her mood nor the rest of the day. So, I pushed the lingering memory of my dream to the back of my mind and got prepared for Benjamin's arrival. By the time I was finished I felt much better.

Benjamin seemed to have impeccable timing that morning. As I made my way to the front door to leave, I saw him approach through the doors window. I looked at myself in the mirror momentarily as he knocked on the door. My reflection stared back at me. Full veiled as if I were hiding from the world. Hiding even from myself in fact.

It had been awhile since I last saw my reflection without the veil. I stood and dared myself to take a look. To take in what I was hiding from everyone. If only as just a reminder. I felt it would be good for myself. Despite that as I slowly began to remove the veil, I lost the courage that I had only seconds prior mustard up.

I paused briefly in doubt. My inner voice daring me to be courageous. Just as I submitted to that voice and began to remove the veil Benjamin knocked on the door once more and gave me a startled. I took that interruption as an escape from the inevitable. Instead of facing that demon that morning I opened the door and greeted Benjamin.

"Well good morning beautiful," he said before I could get out a word.

His words gave me instant comfort. It was exactly what I needed to hear in that moment. It made me forget about my dream I had that night. It also made me forget about the haunting distance I felt growing between my sister and me. It even made me forget about my standoff with my bittersweet secret. The secret I knew I would have to share at some point.

"I got these for you," Benjamin went on as he handed me a bouquet of Tulips.

He then gave a modest head knob accompanied by his intoxicating smile as he reached out for my hand. Butterflies filled my stomach as I obliged. He had a way of giving me butterflies in my tummy often. In fact, I cannot recall one time that we have been together were he did not have that effect on me at least once. Quite often more than once per visit.

He could not see my smile behind the veil. However, I am sure he knew it was there. It was written in my eyes. As always.

"Shall we," he suggested as he led the way to the car, he had waiting on us.

Still lost for words I just followed. When we made it to the car Benjamin grabbed the door for me. Before I got into the car, I turned to him and admired the man he was. A gentleman indeed. I thought to myself father would have liked him. I also admired the fact that coincidentally he got me tulips. I wanted to kiss him but reframed and instead proceeded to enter the car. As I turned to enter Benjamin took hold of my hand to grab my attention.

"Wait," he said as I turned back to him. "I forgot to give you something," he went on wearing an intoxicating glare.

He then proceeded to kiss me through the veil once more. Only this time I did not resist nor panic. I could feel his passion through the thin cloth that separated our lips from flesh to flesh contact. The kiss sent a warm sensation throughout my entire body. Particularly there was a warm magical feeling experienced in my lady region. A unique feeling, I had yet to experience.

The kiss was brief yet monumental. We both lingered in its charm. Our heads passionately rested pressed together. His hands gently holding my cheeks. When Benjamin did finally back away from the kiss, I noticed his skin was redden and his smile even brighter.

"There, now we can go," He said as he assisted me into the car. He then entered the car himself and called out to the driver, "To the meeting now kind Sir."

And just like that we were off into motion. The car ride was silent but brief. I admired my tulips and Benjamin stared out the window. Occasionally he would look to me and give a warm smile. I assumed he was deep in thought. Consumed by what to expect at his father's final will decree reading.

I wanted to comfort him. However, I honestly did not know how. So, I did the best I could. I took his hand into mine and kissed it. Then I looked him directly into his eyes and told him,

"I am here for you Benjamin... I truly am here for you."

He smiled and then kissed my hand. Then he reached up and wiped a tear that had begun to fall from my left eye. I had become emotional and had not realized. It was then when I knew that I had absolutely fallen for Benjamin. When I realized that his pain and suffering was mine and vice versa.

He stared deep into my eyes and for the first time he said those magical words, "I love you Desire."

Honestly, his words did not catch me by surprise. In fact, I could feel his love long before he ever spoke those words. It radiated from him and surrounded me like a blanket of comfort and security. When he spoke those words though they just about melted my heart. For I too felt the same.

Without hesitation those words fell from my mouth like a mighty water over a grand fall. As I stared off into the man of my dream's eyes smitten by his confession of love. I eagerly reciprocated.

"I love you too Benjamin," I confessed boldly.

Then simultaneously in absolute synchronicity we both confessed, "I have known since the first day we met."

Our synchronized confession gave us both a chuckle. We shared a joyful laugh as the vehicle came to a halt in front of a mystic looking castle. It looked like something out of a fairytale. It had a grand gesture very similar to Cypress Hill. I remember thinking that if buildings were somehow lineage related then surely this one was a sibling of Cypress Hill.

The castle was surrounded by a grand wall. The wall looked as if it was made of solid gold blocks. The blocks seemed to stretch effortlessly around the castle's vast perimeter. As we approahed the walls door it puzzled my reasoning because it was a sequoia tree.

The tree must have stood over three hundred feet tall. Its circumference well over one hundred fifty feet. The tree stood there majestically as if it had been there since the beginning of all time. The sight of it took my breath away. It truly was remarkable.

When I turned to Benjamin to validate my reasoning he seemed just as stunned as I. Momentarily I was a bit puzzled as to how we would enter the tree considering I did not see an entry. Then right before my eyes the tree's trunk parted a pathway. Unhesitant the driver began to drive through the path the trees set before us. As he did the tree's path closed behind us and appeared to swallow us whole.

When we reached the other side, something happened. It felt as if all my troubles that burdened me were lifted from my shoulders. All I felt was love, peace, and happiness. I felt as if somehow, I was exactly where I needed to be in that moment. From the look on Benjamin face I would say he felt the same.

We were both overwhelmed with joy as the car kept driving up the long drive that led up to the castle. The view was stunning. It was as if we had driven right into a magical mystical land. A giant forest where all the trees were as large as the one at the gate or larger. Somehow, they seemed to be alive.

I could feel the trees gossiping amongst one another about our presence. The thought of it gave me a euphoric tickle inside. I began to laugh uncontrollably. I guess that saying that laughter is contagious is true because Benjamin began to laugh as well. Shortly after him the driver also began to laugh.

The car was filled with laughter as it approached the massive castle. It was as if we were drunk on joy. It was the most peaceful feeling I had ever felt. By the time the car came to a halt in front of the castle I had just about laughed myself silly. Then just like that the laughter stopped.

We all peered up at the castle in awe. Not quite sure what to expect next. Despite our uncertainty the driver got out of the car and made his way to Benjamin's door.

"Well, here we are sir," He called out as Benjamins door swung open.

"Thank you, kind Sir," Benjamin replied promptly as he stood to his feet.

Still feeling the buzz from my laughing fit I found it difficult to remove the smile from my face. I saw that Benjamin was also still wearing his as he made his way to my door. This gave me a bit of comfort and eased the weary feeling that had settled in the pit of my belly. By the time he had reached my door I was more than eager to join him.

"My lady please join me," Benjamin insisted as my door swung open.

He then reached up for my hand and assist me out of the car. First thing I noticed once out of the car was booth the Sun and the Moon shined in the sky above the castle. They booth shined as if it were their peaks. As if they were on a date romancing one another. As bizarre as it may sounds, I could feel the love that they had for one another.

"Shall we," Benjamin called out to capture my attention as he began to lead us up the stairs to the castle door.

As we approached the door, I could faintly hear the sound of a piano playing. I smelled the scent of fresh

Jasmine and could taste cinnamon in the air. My body began to feel as if the wind was giving me a massage. Just the mere thought of a drink quince my thirst and that of food my hunger. The thought of pleasure pleased me and that of comfort, comforted.

How could it be I selfishly thought to myself? What was this place I had found myself? Once we were at the door Benjamin lifted his fist to knock but as he did the door opened before he could. We looked at one another then back at the driver to find he nor the car was there. Instead only the giant forest was there staring and gossiping at and about us.

So, we ignored the obvious anxiety that had begun to settle in and entered the castle. The doors seemed to close behind us as the castle's grand foyer illuminated to our presence. The foyer seemed to stretch forward endlessly. In the distance headed our way there was a man wearing a tuxedo and top hat. He whistled and upbeat tone and tap his walking stick to the ground to the beat.

Benjamin and I did not think much of it. In fact, we were happy to see the man. We assumed he was the person we had come to meet. Peculiar enough despite how long the hallway was the man made it to us rather quickly. It was almost as if he teleported up the hallway.

"Well, you to have arrived," the man called out as he extended his hand to Benjamin. "My name is Maxwell Whimper-Nickel though everyone calls me Max," He went on in a chipper tone.

Benjamin hand quickly met with Max's to oblige his gesture of greetings.

"The pleasure is all mine Max I'm Benjamin and this lovely lady is Desire," Benjamin replied humbly.

"Well, I suppose the two of you are a bit tired and perhaps parched to say the least. So, without further ado please allow me to show you to your quarters where you can get freshened up and perhaps get a nap in prior to super," Max insisted as he began to lead us up the hall from which he had come.

"Well, to be quite honest Max I was hoping that this business of ours would not be so prolonged if you do understand," Benjamin explained as he and I followed behind Max.

"Prolonged you say," Max called out as he came to an abrupt halt before turning to Benjamin and me. "Well, I see your concern Benjamin and I assure you our business will be everything but prolonged as you call it," Max went on before bursting out in a tedious laugh. "Now do follow and hurry along for we have a tight schedule ahead of ourselves," Max continued as he turned and continued up the hallway.

Though it felt as if we had only taken a few steps we had reached our destination. When I turned back to look behind us the hallway stretched on endlessly. It left me a bit confused. However, before I could rationalize with the idea of it Max open the door to our quarters, and I was left speechless.

"Well, here we are the master's quarters," Max yelled out ending with a bit of a giggle.

Benjamin and I could not believe our eyes. Looking into the quarters was like looking into a kingdom of its own.

"Do enjoy," Max called out from behind us.

"There is one thing," Benjamin attempted to ask as he turned to Max only to find he was no longer there.

The two of us looked at one another confused of where Max had gone so quickly.

"I suppose we better get some rest it has been a long drive up and I am really trying to wrap my mind around what's going on here," Benjamin suggested. "Shall we my lady," he went on as he gestured me to enter the quarters first.

I happily obliged.

Chapter 5

A Palace for Two

I know what you are thinking. Let us hear more about that bed chambers that resembled a palace of its own. Well, that was no overstatement. That bed chamber was magically miraculous. Upon walking through the door, it was as if we step out of one world and into another. Much like the day I met Benjamin.

Instead of walking into a bedroom we stepped into a field of flowers species unknown. If I had to take a guess, I would say they were a cross between tulips and lilies. My two favorite flowers of all time. These peculiar flowers comprised the entire field that seemed to stretch out endlessly in every direction. To both our amazement the flowers animated and began to sing, "Row Row Row Your Boat" upon acknowledgement of our presence.

The key they sang in was angelic and its harmonic frequency filled us with euphoria. It was as if we had fell under their trance. A trance of absolute bliss. It seemed as if the flowers somehow knew that we had fell under their trance. For once we were under, they parted and revealed a golden pathway that navigated through to the horizon. Where at the end of the horizon the Sun stood still.

It was as if the Sun was standing before us luring us in towards its direction. Patiently awaiting our arrival or anxiously our demise. Still enchanted by the flowers Benjamin and I began to follow the path unconsciously. I recall being on foot when we started down the path. However, not long into the journey somehow, we were no longer on foot. Instead, we found ourselves in what appeared to be an old miners rail cart barreling down a track headed straight for the Sun.

I found myself stuck in a place between abstract thought and realism. How was it possible that we were experiencing what we were? Was it all as the flower's song implied only but a dream? As I ponder the validity of the current occurrences the flowers stop singing and began to cheer as the barreling cart grew closer to the Sun. Benjamin stood to the amazement at the front of the cart staring down the Sun as if he hadn't a care in the world.

Something had come over him. His demeanor of courage while staring down the unknown was contagious and gave me a sense of relief. All my anxiety dissipated as he began to sing at the front of the cart. All I heard was his fearless voice singing, "Knocking on Heavens Door," as if it were to the Sun. It was in that moment of serenity I too had the urge to sing along. So, I did just that. As did the flowers.

It was in that moment of synchronicity that the cart collided with the Sun. The most peculiar thing about it was rather than being disintegrated into a pile of ash we drove straight through it. Even more peculiar when we emerged on the other side we were no longer in the old miner's cart. Instead, we were now in what appeared to be a hot air balloon soaring through a night sky full of stars. The experience was truly magical.

The term took my breath away would be an understatement for what we experienced. My heart was pounding from exhilaration and my mind raced in every imaginable direction. The only thing I could wrap my mind around was being closer to Benjamin. He stood on the opposite side of the Balloon's carriage staring at me as I stared back at him. He looked just as thrilled as I was and with good reason. He even had a hint of disbelief etched in his facial expression similar to my own.

I knew he needed to be close to me as well. Without over thinking it I made my way to him. I wanted to share that moment of shock and disbelief, so I took his hand and placed it on my chest. From underneath my hand that held his against my chest firmly I could feel my heartbeat.

Benjamin smiled as he took my other hand and placed it against his chest.

The beats of our hearts were in sync. It felt as if they were one. The magic of that moment shall never be erased from memory. In fact, we lingered there in that moment. Clarifying its significance to ourselves and the cosmos.

The cosmos had its own personal way of gratifying our special moment. It presented us with the most spectacular exhibit. A stellar Nebula in the not so distant distance. What a sight for the eyes. We were allowed to eyewitness the birth of a Star.

Caught in the magic of the moment Benjamin did the unthinkable. Before I could stop him, he removed the veil of my head dress and ran his hand across my face.

"Absolutely stunning," Benjamin called out before going in for a kiss.

I honestly did not know how to respond. How could I have let this happen? What was I thinking letting my guard down? I was succumbed to the moment and surely now that moment had reached its end. Those were the thoughts that bombarded my mind following Benjamin's bold gesture of affection.

His kiss though soothing momentarily went unrecognized. I mean, I did feel the soft sensation of his lips actually pressed against mine for the first time. I also felt the tickle of his mustache on my top lip which sent a chilling sensation throughout my entire body. I even felt his tongue as it passive aggressively tried to pry its way into my mouth. His hands pressed against both sides of my face.

Yes, it is true I felt all of these things. They all felt amazing. In fact, it was the fact that I was feeling them that was most surprising. How was it possible? Why hadn't I repulsed Benjamin with my hideous disfigurement?

It was the answer to that question that I longed. Did I dare to reach up and confront the elephant in the room? I knew that it was a must. It was the only way that I would feel comfortable with myself in that moment. So, I followed in Benjamin's bold lead and reached up and slid my hands underneath his to touch my face.

My hands were the first to relief when they arrived at my face and felt skin that was as smooth as a baby's bottom. I let off a sigh of relief and surrender to Benjamin's passion. My sigh must have distracted him.

"Is everything alright my love," Benjamin asked in a concerned tone?

I was hesitant to respond. Mainly because I was still trying to wrap my mind around the miraculous disappearance of my life long burdensome scars. I quickly gathered myself with hopes not the sour our moment.

"Yes, everything is just fine... Perfect in fact," I replied followed by a bright smile.

Just as I did a shooting star blazed pass the balloon. It was so close it looked as if I could have reached out and taken hold to it. Benjamin's eyes lit up with thrill.

"Wow... did you see that," he asked?

I smiled and quickly made my way over to the edge of the balloon carriage to get a better look. Benjamin eagerly followed. When he arrived, he took me into his arms from behind and the two of us admired the view. We saw all sorts of wonders in the sky that night. Many indescribable by words.

One occasion in particular took me by surprise. We reached a point in the night sky where all the stars somehow turned into what appeared to be bubbles. Within those bubbles were snippets of my life. Some filled with my most intimate moments. Others filled with my darkest moments.

Of all the moments that were present a recent one caught my attention. It was the dream I had of my father. The dream I tried to hold on to the most. We were there standing in the field as we were in the dream. I saw myself tempted but afraid to look up at my father. Afraid of the uncertainty and the possible upset if it were not him.

For some reason I really connected to myself in that moment. I believe it was because I wanted to be there again with my father. Then the unthinkable occurred. As I willed my desire, I felt myself project there. Though my physical body was still in the hot air balloon with Benjamin, I had also become myself in that dream.

I stood before my father still feeling the anxiety I felt in the dream. However, this time I knew the man that stood before me was my father. I also knew that I did not have much time with him. So, rather than being bashful or confused by what was occurring I decided to seize the moment.

"Father I have missed you so much," I professed as I threw myself into his arms. "Why... Why did you ...," I made out before father interrupted.

It was as if he knew what I was going to ask and avoided the answer. Perhaps he felt I could not handle the truth. Or maybe he did not want me to have the truth due to being afraid of what I may do with it. Whatever the case was he knew he had to address the matter. That he did.

"Desire... sweetheart... nothing is as it seems," Father said as he caressed the back of my head.

With my head now buried in his chest I began to weep. His comforting caress still as soothing as it was when I was just a child. It reminded me of old times. Though they were so far ago. They seemed very close indeed.

I anxiously awaited my father's continuance of his explanation. Still confused and haunted by the idea of him taking his own life. I had to know there was a meaning to it all. Perhaps, then I could finally let go and move forward. Or even better; understand.

"It was my time Desire," father continued voice echoing from deep within his chest. "I had reached an end point in our timeline that you know of," He went on.

"Our timeline," I asked curiously? "What do you mean father," I continued?

"Sweetheart... just know when one thing ends in one place it begins in another," Father explained passionately.

He then pulled me from his chest and stared down into my eyes. He gave me the look that he often did when I was a child. His solemn look of reassurance. I knew that it was his way of assuring me that everything would be just fine. So, I accepted his gesture at face value.

Though the answer father gave was vague; it did suffice. I admit I did not know how to comprehend it. However, I knew that over time its true meaning would become a revelation. The idea of that gave me peace of mind. I felt like I could in fact move forward. Knowing that father was just fine and that I would be as well.

I smiled up at father to assure him that I was reassured. He reciprocated with an optimistic smile. Then the two of us shared an embrace. I felt myself again hoping our time together would never end. Though, I knew that its end was a certainty.

Then just as swiftly as I was projected to that moment with my father; it had come and gone. I was now back where I belonged. In that mysterious hot air balloon with Benjamin. It was him embracing me now instead of my father. Not only was I fine with that. I also found great comfort in it.

His masculine arms wrapped firmly around mine. My head buried in his chest nestled beneath his chin. His heartbeat as soothing as a cool breeze on a hot summer day. His alluring scent of bergamot, oakmoss and labdanum all collectively played its role in seducing me that night.

I felt an urge like no other to be with Benjamin in that moment. My heart raced from both excitement and anxiety. My hands slowly made their way behind Benjamin's head. I caressed his ears to express my passion along the way. Then I pulled him in for a kiss.

Without hesitation Benjamin eagerly reciprocated. My kiss of submission ignited a blazing fire of passion between the two of us. Our passion then grew faster than a patch of wild bamboo. The kiss quickly evolved as Benjamin for the first time removed my headdress. As it fell from me, I felt liberated.

It was Benjamin's lips that pulled my attention from my moment of liberation. As they departed from mine and made their way to my neck I was consumed by anticipation. When his lips sensually made contact a desirable chill raced throughout my entire being. My knees buckled and I fell into his seductive embrace.

He then gently led my virgin body down to the floor of the vessel. It was there where our clothes seamless disappearance both fascinated and encouraged. Staring into my eyes and I into his it was in that moment we knew we belonged together. It was in that moment we both let go and allowed fate to take its due course.

Chapter 6

Mystic Harbor

The next morning when I woke up, I found myself lying in bed back in that magical bed chambers. Though I was still wrapped in Benjamins arms I was a bit confused. I remembered very distinctly the things that took place the previous night. I mean, how could I forget. After all, that was the night I officially became a woman.

I could still feel the tingling sensation in my vagina. The recollection of Benjamin's kisses all over my body gave me chills. My knight in shining armor. Everything I longed for he had thus far given and more.

As I laid there trying to rationalize with what I experienced I realized it must have been a dream. How was I now back in bed? Though the bed was a delight I would much rather had been back in that mystical vessel. As I released a sigh of disappointment and relief, I pulled the silk linen to cover my bashful face.

To my dismay, I discovered my head dress was missing. Out of sheer panic I frantically darted out of bed and made my way to the bathroom. Just as fast as I entered, I slammed the door shut behind me. My heart was racing, and a lump of anxiety had formed in my throat. Not only was my head dress missing I was also completely naked.

What did this mean? Had last night actually occurred and if so, how was it possible? Out of curiosity I slowly reached my hands up to my face. Just before they made contact, I paused. I was afraid to face the reality of the situation even though I knew it was a must.

An awkward silence filled the room. I wrestled with the idea of confronting my curiosity. It was in that moment I caught a glimpse of the mirror across the room. The mirror seemed to challenge me to confront it. As I stood with my back pressed up against the bathroom door, I dared myself to walk over to the mirror.

Then with a burst of vigor I forced myself to make a move. As I began to make my way to the mirror a familiar voice interrupted my courage.

"Desire, sweetheart... is everything okay," Benjamin called out in a concerned tone?

All the commotion must have wakened Him. Hesitant to respond I stood in silence staring down the door then back at the mirror. I heard Benjamin get out of bed and began to make his way over to the bathroom. My heart raced from anxiety. Rather than respond I froze like a deer in headlights.

"Desire," Benjamin called out once more as his footsteps grew closer. "Is everything okay beautiful," He went on?

I knew I had to make a move, so I did just that. I closed my eyes and began to make my way to the mirror. Just as I stepped from the door, I felt it began to open. Benjamin called out once more.

"Desire?"

Out of reflex I flung my body up against the door forcing it shut. I desperately wanted to prevent Benjamin from entering. I could not let him see me. Heck, I was not even sure I wanted to see me. Though, I knew I had to.

I quickly turned the skeleton key that dangled from the door to lock it. Then I slowly backed away from the door. I felt a slight relief, but it was short lived interrupted by Benjamin's voice.

"Sweetheart, I am a bit confused, did I do something wrong," Benjamin asked in a concerned tone? "Can you please help me understand how I can make things right," He went on?

I knew I owed him an explanation but what could I say?

"Oh, just a minute sweetheart I am fine," I called out from sheer reflex.

The doorknob shimmied. Then followed a gentle shake of the door. My heart reached the point where it was no longer racing but now instead stood still. The room began to feel as if all the walls had begun to close in on me. My mental capacity was consumed by two parameters. That which lies before me, the door. Then, that which lies behind me, the mirror.

"Desire, I want you to know I really enjoyed last night," Benjamin explained in a compassionate tone. "I mean… you are everything I have ever wanted," He went one. "You are definitely the woman I have been chasing around my dreams," He continued. "Arguably, the most beautiful woman I have ever seen," Benjamin professed passionately.

It was Benjamins voice that pulled my mind from a consumed state. His voice paired with the words he was saying captivated my mind. He had confirmed that last night and all of its magic actually occurred. He had also, confirmed my beauty. The idea of that gave me the strength I needed to boldly confront the mirror. So, I did.

I could see my reflection as I approached the mirror. The closer I got the clearer my reflection grew. Then, there I was standing before myself. I could not believe my eyes. It was the first time I had seen myself. I mean, really saw myself. I was beautiful.

As I stood speechless admiring myself in the mirror, I became emotional. A dream come true is what I was experiencing. How could it be I thought to myself briefly? I ran my hand across my face and was overwhelmed with joy. My skin was as clear and as smooth as silk.

I was so enthused by my new skin I decided to draw myself a bath. As the water filled the bath, I continued to admire myself. Honestly, I could not stop looking at myself. My smooth silky skin, olive colored and blemish free. This brought a smile to my face.

Over the sound of the running water I heard Benjamin began to sing. His voice was accompanied by a guitar. Both equally soothing however, Benjamin's voice stood out.

"Baby I been trying to tell you... That if you are tired of being alone.... All you got to do is call me ... and I'll be there," Benjamin sang proudly.

I felt my mind gravitate towards the song Benjamin sang. It was the song from last night. A duet. Inspired by Benjamins chivalry, I instinctively chimed in.

"Honey I am so glad you told me.... Exactly how you really do feel...

Cause honey I been wanting to call you.... Please get here....

The guitar chords took over in the absence of our voices. Moved by the passion of the moment I felt a strong desire to be with Benjamin. I made my way to the door that stood between us. I unlocked the door with a gentle turn of the skeleton key then turned the knob to open it. As the door slowly swung open giving Benjamin an invitation to join me, I made my way to the bath.

When I turned to enter the bath, I saw Benjamin entering the room. He was still strumming the guitar as he made his way to me. Once to me, he attempted to sing the next bar of the song. However, my lips met his before he could.

Our passion rapidly escalated. In-between our kisses, Benjamin set the guitar to the side revealing his nakedness. It was very obvious that he was more than excited in that moment. Even more obvious was my own desire and excitement levels. I could not keep my lips off of him. As he entered the tub to join me my kisses never stopped.

Then there, in the middle of the tub the two of us let go. We allowed one another to enjoy each other in its entirety. Time seemed to become nonexistent. Our passion stretched on prolonged and intoxicating.

Hours must have gone by before our connection was interrupted. There was a knock at the door accompanied by a familiar voice.

"Mr. & Mrs. Whip, I must inform you that your presence is required, "The butler called out through the door. "Please report to the Main Hall at your earliest convenience," The Butler continued.

Benjamin was the first to give attention to the situation. As he got out of the bath to address the door a note slide underneath. He picked up the note up and read its contents while I admired what a handsome man he was. I was completely smitten. One may even suggest love is what I was experiencing.

"Well beautiful, I guess we better get to it," Benjamin suggested as he made his way back over to me. He then took me into his arms and carried me to the bed. As he laid me onto the bed, I kissed his lips and tried to seduce him.

"Sweetheart, though I really want this... and trust me I do... we really should get going," Benjamin made out through my kisses.

"Okay, if you feel you can walk away from all this then fine," I said wearing a flirtatious grin.

I will admit, part of me was hoping Benjamin could not walk away. When he tried to, I grew uneasy momentarily. To my good fortune, he was being charmingly cunning. He did not get but a few steps before he turned back. He could not resist me nor could I him.

It was late afternoon when we finally made it to the Main Hall. When we arrived, the Butler was there anxiously waiting to escort us to the meeting with Benjamin's father attorney.

"Right this way Sir," the Butler called out as he began to swiftly lead the way up a long hallway. "Mr. Lester has been very patient with your tardiness so, please let's put some pep in our step shall we," the Butler rambled on in an agitated tone. "You would think you would be excited to get to this meeting I mean it's not every day a man inherits a large fortune and the opportunity of a lifetime," the Butler continued under his breath.

Benjamin and I look at one another baffled by the Butlers demeanor.

"Okay here we are Sir, right through those doors your destiny awaits you," the Butler instructed as he extended his arm out to guide Benjamin through the grandiose double doors we now stood in front of.

Benjamin turned to me took my hand and started through the door.

"Umm, just a moment," the Butler called out as he extended his arm in front of me as to put a halt to me entering the room.

"This is unfortunately a by invite only meeting, He continued now catching Benjamin's attention as well.

"Excuse me," Benjamin called out as he turned to address the situation.

"Umm, unfortunately Sir this meeting is supposed to be by invite only," the Butler explained pulling Benjamin to the side in an effort to create privacy.

"Well, unfortunately kind sir there is nothing private between me and this woman," Benjamin interjected sternly. She goes where I go so please, stand aside," Benjamin continued as he reached out and grabbed my hand again. "Shall we," Benjamin looked over and asked?

I smiled in admiration and followed his lead. As we entered, I saw a tall slender man standing behind a desk wearing a skittish smile. He was well groomed and dressed. However, his suit looked as if it were a couple sizes too big. As we approached him, I noticed his skin was extremely pale and freckles covered his face.

I got the feeling that something was off with the guy. I mean his lips were oddly thin, and he wore a big red mustache that practically hid his entire top lip. His eyes were stone cold blue, and he had a stare that could wake the dead.

"Hello, Mr. Whip, he yelped out followed by a raspy smokers cough. "Come in, come in, it is a pleasure to see you," he continued as he extended his hand out to Benjamin to greet him.

Benjamin eagerly reciprocated extending his hand out delivering a solid shake.

"How do you do kind Sir," Benjamin asked politely.

"I am fine young man please have a seat now," the man instructed Benjamin and me.

He cleared his throat which triggered another episode of smoker's cough before continuing.

"You will have to forgive this darn cough I don't know what the heck is causing it," the man explained to Benjamin and me. "My name is Franco Lester, your father's long-standing attorney," he went on. "Your father was a very close and dear friend to me, and his presence will surely be missed," Franco professed before pulling out his handkerchief and blowing his nose.

He appeared to be grieving over the loss of Benjamin's father. The room filled with silence as Franco gathered his bearings. For a brief period in the room it felt as everything stood still. It was so void in the room I could hear my own heartbeat. I respected the silence.

It was Benjamin's voice that disrupted it.

"I'm sorry Sir, for your loss," Benjamin said compassionately.

"Oh, don't be silly it is I that am sorry for your loss young man," Franco quickly rebutted. "Now where was I, that's right just about to hand the keys to the fortress over to you," Franco said humorous tone followed by a flimsy chuckle.

"The keys to the fortress," Benjamin asked wearing a puzzled look?

"Yes, the fortress, all of what you see here... and more.... Much... much... more," Franco explained.

"Is that so," Benjamin asked in a skeptical tone?

"Yes, that is so.... your father left it all to you," Franco insisted. "All I need is your John Hancock right here and I shall be out of your hair leaving you to enjoy your new life... and might I say what a lovely life it is," Franco suggested confidently as he turned a thick contract toward Benjamin and extended out a pen.

"What's the catch here.... I mean... all this is just mine now," Benjamin asked in a confused tone? "Was my father like in the mafia or something.... I mean where did all this...

fortune come from," Benjamin continued as he reached for the pen?

Franco quickly pulled back the pen and gave Benjamin a stern stare right into his eyes.

"Your father was a master.... Just know that my boy," Franco explained in an animated tone before winking his left eye. "Now... your signature already please," He went on as he extended the pen to Benjamin once more.

Benjamin hesitantly took the pen gave a quick glare at the contract and proceeded to sign his name.

"Well now, and just like that your abode awaits you," Franco said now wearing a satisfied smile. "If you would I would like to gather my belongings here and see myself on my merry way but please do enjoy yourselves," Franco rambled out as he aggressively stood to his feet and escorted us back to the door in which we had come from.

As Benjamin and I began to exit the room Franco turned and headed back to his desk.

"I almost forgot.... One las thing I must explain to you before you depart please Sir," Franco called out catching our attention. "If you would please this will just take a moment Sir," He went on.

We turned around and headed towards him and made a few steps before he chimed in again.

"Just the Master for this bit of news sweetheart I truly am sorry," Franco explained. "Of course, If you would be so kind to join me for an audience alone Master, He went on now addressing Benjamin as Master.

Benjamin looked over at me then back at Franco. Before he could object Franco chimed in again.

"I assure you it will be brief, and it is of the utmost importance kind sir,"

"It's fine gone a head I will be right outside the door," I said encouraging Benjamin to accept the private audience with Franco.

"You sure," Benjamin asked?

"Yes, I am sure... it is fine I will be right here waiting ... go on now," I insisted.

"Okay, I am right inside here if you need me, Benjamin ensured me then planted a kiss on my lips before joining Franco.

Once Benjamin entered Franco gave the door a nudge to shut it. The door gave off a loud screech before closing briefly then slightly reopening. I was not trying to, but I could hear their discussion through the door. I could not make out everything they were saying but I caught glimpses of it.

One thing in particular caught my attention. Franco told Benjamin that the two of us were in between whatever that meant. I was not really sure how to make sense of it. As Franco tried to explain it to Benjamin it sounded like something out of a science fiction novel. Something about a rare opportunity when two worlds intertwine.

The thought of it made me feel uneasy. I can sense that Benjamin felt the same way. When he returned to me, he had a weird look in his eyes. He looked as if he had something to tell me but was not sure how.

"Is everything okay my love," I asked in a concerned tone?

He was hesitant to answer. It was as if whatever he was told weighed heavy on his mind.

"Oh, um... yes everything is fine," Benjamin forced out in a confident tone. "I have something I want to show you... Come on now don't you worry your fancy young lady," Benjamin continued wearing a smile bright enough to erase all the darkness in the world.

He took my hand a we darted off down a hall and did not stop until we reached the front door. We keep right on up the drive to about halfway then took off through the rose garden.

"Come on, keep up young lady," Benjamin looked back and demanded playfully.

I smiled and tried to keep up the best I could. Then in a distance I began to see it. There it was. That magical balloon from last night. The sight of it filled me with exhilaration. I could hardly stand it.

Something took over me and I began to run as hard and as fast as I could. My spontaneous explosion of speed caught Benjamin off guard, and I was able to put some distance between us. Once he realized what had happened, he reciprocated and gave chase behind me.

"I'm going to catch you, young lady," Benjamin yelled out accompanied by laughter.

I looked back and noticed he quickly began to catch up to me. Honestly, in that moment I wanted him to catch me. I wanted to be back in his arms and on that magical balloon. In fact, there was no other place I wanted to be. So, with a big scream I deliberately slowed down.

Within seconds I was apprehended. Nestled tightly in Benjamins arms where I belonged. Subdued with passion Benjamin went in for a kiss. My body unconsciously complied. It wanted to be taken. It even gets better, that Magical Balloon stood before us.

I knew in the back of my mind a magical night was certain. I also knew that this new life that we had been given was in a sense magical itself. Everything we wanted or needed had been provided. It truly was a blessing; despite not knowing what I had done to be so deserving.

So, I pushed all the doubt out of my mind and surrendered completely to the moment. I surrendered myself completely to Benjamin as well. Then while still kissing me Benjamin lifted me into his mighty arms and boarded the magical vessel. The vessel seemed to consciously respond to our presence and began to ascend. A night of love and bliss had begun.

Chapter 7

Fate

When I woke the next morning, I could not recall much of the previous night. However, one thing was certain, it must have been amazing. I could see the morning sky overhead upon opening my eyes. The Sun was starting to peer through a cluster of clouds. Its warmth was very soothing against my skin that was exposed as

Benjamin and I laid naked on the floor of that magical vessel.

Though calmed by the sensation of being wrapped in Benjamins arms, I was a bit disoriented. When his eyes opened and met with mine, I sensed he felt the same.

"Morning my love," he greeted as he sat up and ran a finger through my hair.

His finger started at the corner of my ear and seductively slid around it, and down my neck sending goose bumps across my entire body. His finger stopped at the base of my neck. Then there, accompanied by the rest of his hand, pulled me in for a kiss. The kiss was alluring and enticed my desire for him. I could not contain my passion. I was intoxicated by lust.

I submissively surrendered my body to his will. My mind to his essence. My soul to his soul. We intertwined in genius culminating instantaneously. Simultaneously, his kisses trailed across my body. His caress opened my heart. His thrust... sent me into that place. His passion truly was a gesture of reciprocation.

We lost track of time. Hours must have passed. The morning had begun to fade long before we finally had the strength to pull ourselves from satisfaction. I cannot find the words to adequately explain how great I felt after our encounter that morning. Benjamin... was my hero.

The two of us had worked up an appetite so we decided to get up and get some food. To our surprise, our magical vessel had landed in a mysterious place. Neither of us was sure exactly where we were. However, we both were amazed by its beauty.

We quickly clothed ourselves eager to explore this new land. Benjamin was the first off the vessel. He then turned to me, took me into his arms and began to walk. His macho gesture flattering in nature gave me a tickle.

" Oh my... what great strength you have, "I suggested playfully before planting a kiss on his lips.

It was to know surprise to me when he decided to carry me for miles. Nestled in his arms embraced by his protection I received a grand tour of this new land. What a wondrous land it was indeed. The two of us saw all types of strange and mind provoking things.

We saw a one-legged elephant that looked as if it is one leg was actually comprised of four normal elephant legs fused together. The sight of it baffled the both of us, Benjamin the most, however. His only way of conceptualizing the creature was to name it. So, he did. He called it a Legaphant as to show it belonging to the elephant family while acknowledging its significant difference: that elephant's leg.

We saw a mountain that floated in the sky detached from the ground below. We marveled at its beauty for hours as its enchantment enticed us to reach it. That we did. We found a chain of mini floating mountains in comparison to it. The mini mountains spiraled around it majestically leading to its peak.

Once at the top, what we found defied all logic. It was a waterfall that instead of falling ascended high into the sky. It extended well beyond what our vision allowed us to see. It was the beauty of it that made us decide to make camp there for the night. We just could not leave the presence of such a marvel.

I remember a distinct feeling that came over me in its' presence. It felt as if I were in the presence of the essence of existence itself. I could not stop wrestling with the notion in the back of my mind, how was it possible? Where were we? Why was it so that Benjamin and I had been privileged to witness such a thing?

I began to recall a story my father told me. The story of my mother's and his encounter with Mystic Harbor. I once considered that story the stretch of the imagination. Now, I could no longer deny the validity of my father's words. Realizing that his words were in fact a fact, I was compelled to explore our camp site.

Benjamin had already began trying to make the camp cozy by gathering wood for a fire. While he worked on that I decided to poke around and see what other marvels I would stumble upon. I called out to him to let him know of my intentions,

"Benjamin darling, I am going to just poke around a bit to see if maybe I can find us something to eat."

"My love, please be careful and don't wonder off to far," Benjamin replied as I made my way towards the setting Sun.

It silently called to me as it began to disappear behind the horizon. Though it set off in the distance its light radiated as if it was only and arm's length away. The warmth it gave off soothed my skin. The hue that began to unfold was like nothing I had ever seen before. Even more spectacular I not only saw the vibrant colors I also heard them.

There were seven vibrant colors that appeared. Each of which gave off a harmonic frequency. The sensation of the tones seemed to pierce my psyche. I began to feel lightheaded as a distinct ringing began to buzz in my head. Then everything went black.

At first, I thought I had passed out unconscious. However, I quickly ruled that out because despite now being submerged in complete darkness I could still feel my awareness. Then I heard a voice call out to me,

"Welcome Desire..."

"Whose there," I quickly called out?

"Fear not young one for you are now amongst the Masters," the voice called out.

"The Masters.... but wait, I do not understand.... What Masters," I asked frantically?

"The ascended Masters, Lords of the rays," The voice called out.

"Lords of the rays... But why... how is this possible," I asked now confused by what was taking place.

"Desire, you have reached a pinnacle point of evolution and there is a choice soon to be made," The voice professed.

"A choice... What choice," I asked anxiously?

"Go now young one... we shall reconvene soon," the voice proclaimed.

Then there was a familiar voice calling my name. It was Benjamin.

"Desire, wait..., Benjamin yelped out in a panic.

I was not sure why Benjamin was in such a panic until the darkness was lifted and I found myself stepping off the edge of a cliff. As I began the long descent all I could feel was peace. Though I knew I was falling to an inevitable dark fate, I was not afraid. In fact, I was ready for whatever was to come. I embraced my demise.

I closed my eyes and let go. The wind cradled my now limp body. Fearlessly I welcomed the abyss. I anticipated the collision between me and whatever was below. Then it came.

I felt myself contact something which broke my fall. I was sure it was a rocky patch that had now claimed my life. Then there was nothing. I had entered the void...

"Desire," I heard Benjamin call out.

Then a felt a slight slap on the cheek.

"Wake up love," Benjamin voice called to me again as a few more slight slaps contacted my cheek.

I slowly opened my eyes and I found myself in Benjamins arms. I was still a bit hazy, but something did not feel right. I tried to force myself to gain consciousness.

I could still feel the wind cradling me as if I were still falling. It did not make sense because that would mean Benjamin was falling with me.

That is when I noticed I was not falling but instead, I was soaring. The idea of it caused me to rapidly regain consciousness. When I looked up at Benjamin, he had wings and we were flying.

"Benjamin... what's happening," I asked him now slightly hypnotized by the happenings?

"Don't you worry sweetheart I got you now," He said in a reassuring tone.

The idea of it all was overwhelming. I could not hold on to my brief consciousness. Once again, I was out. It felt like an eternity had passed before I finally came back. When I did, I found myself laying comfortably next to a warm fire. Benjamin was right beside me playing guitar.

When he noticed I had risen, his playing came to an abrupt halt. I could vaguely recall what had just occurred. Benjamin had jumped over the cliff after me. Rather both us meeting our demise, he somehow had wings and flew us to safety.

"Desire are you alright my love," Benjamin said as he came to my aide.

Still a bit taken by it all, rather than meeting his gesture with open arms I resisted. I quickly backed away from his advance to comfort me. My gesture caught him by surprise.

"Desire please don't be afraid sweetheart everything is fine," Benjamin said in a reassuring voice as he continued his advance to comfort me.

"Please, just give me a minute to gather myself," I insisted still resisting his advances of comfort.

"Okay... fine, I guess I owe you at least that," Benjamin agreed resending his notion to comfort me.

Despite all that had taken place there was no denying that I was still in love with Benjamin. He was my knight in shining armor sort of speak. Though now knowing he was somehow apart of all the mystical things that we were experiencing I was growing concerned. Doubt was surely setting in.

I now felt alone and uncertain. As if I was the sole culprit of all the magical experiences. For Benjamin had now started to appear more so as a part of the magic. Rather than experiencing it like I was.

I was unsure exactly what I was experiencing and now felt as if Benjamin had the answers. I was determined to get those answers. So, I turned my attention to Benjamin with that aim in mind.

"Benjamin... none of this is making any sense anymore," I said in a distressed tone. "I mean... how is any of this possible," I went on? "You had wings for crying out loud... Wings Benjamin," I began to rant as the words seem to now spill from my mouth unconsciously. "How do you explain that Benjamin," were the final words that flowed before an absolute silence.

I was now standing, heart racing staring down at Benjamin as he sat with his head low in an attempt to avoid eye contact. I could feel his trouble vibe as he wrestled with the concerns, I had just presented to him. I knew he wanted to relieve himself of the burden of the secrets he was keeping from me.

Then, he did just that. I will admit I was not prepared for what he was about to share. The words he spoke seemed to rip apart my current perception of reality. Though, they did validate the current happenings as being truly mystical. He spoke the words with such prose it captured my undivided attention.

"Desire, please you may want to have a seat," Benjamin insisted "What I am about to tell you may be a bit much to take in," He went on.

He paused and waited for me to comply. I sat across from him. Separating us was the fire still burning bright and vibrate giving off the occasional crackle and pop.

"Well, go on now," I insisted eager to be illumined of the mysteries he was about to reveal.

His eyes seemed to peer out from the fire. His voice, bold and stern. His words, soul bridging. As he began to disclose what he was keeping from me the most peculiar thing occurred. As he spoke, I found myself transcend to the occurrence in which he spoke.

It was the day I met Benjamin. We were there at that coffee boutique only this time things were a bit different. It was I who frantically came into the boutique. I was in a rush because I was to meet Rachel there for breakfast. We were going to discuss me possibly trying to meet someone in the romantic sense.

I admit I was a bit troubled by the idea. Mostly because I did not believe I had much to offer a man in the romantic sense. With my not so charming birth mark and all. What man would even want such mess as his own? These are the types of thoughts that haunted my mind as I entered the boutique.

I was deep in my own thoughts as I made my way into the boutique. I simultaneously dug around in my handbag to get my wallet. As I approached the line to place my order my mind was preoccupied, and I neglected to pay attention to my surroundings. What a poor decision that was on my part.

As it caused me to stumble directly into the waiter causing him to dump an entire tray into the lap of a poor gentleman. The ruckus caused the entire boutique to stall to an abrupt halt. All eyes were on the incident. I was quite embarrassed by the situation. I also felt extremely compassionate for both the gentleman and the waiter who had found themselves spectacles' in the chaos my neglect caused.

In an attempt to mellow things over, I instinctively went into an apologetic gesture of aide.

"Oh, do pardon me kind sirs I am horribly sorry," I called out as I reached down to help the waiter who had fallen to a knee back to his feet.

The gentleman in the booth was the first to respond,

"Not a worry madam," he said as he reached down for my hand and guided me back to my feet.

The first thing I noticed were his eyes. They were hypnotic blue and reminded me of the sea that ran along Cypress Hill. They left me speechless.

"Please, allow me," he went on as he stood to his feet and stepped in to assist the waiter.

Once the waiter was to his feet the gentleman apologized on my behalf.

"Please kind sir, you must forgive this poor woman," The gentleman suggested to the waiter as he dusted himself off and fixed his uniform of sorts. "Now, if you would please join me at a fresh booth madam," the gentleman then turned to me and asked?

I did not know how to respond. I mean, I definitely wanted to say yes. However, I was a bit afraid to say yes and rather embarrassed given the circumstances. So, rather than saying yes, I listened to my gut which was telling me to get out of there.

"I can't... I just can't," I said to the gentleman before bolting for the door.

"Madam... please wait," he called out as he reached out and grabbed for my shoulder in an attempt to catch my attention.

Instead of my shoulder his hands caught hold to my headdress. As I ran from him the force of my thrust and the halt of his grip caused my head dress to strip free. I could feel the garment as it slid from my head publicly unveiling my truth. In a panic I turned back to catch it, but it was too late.

I now stood before the gentleman in rare form. The entire boutique appeared to watch in awe. I felt tears start to tread down my cheeks for I knew my secrete was out. The gentleman stood before me. My headdress in his hand, momentarily speechless along with the rest of the boutique.

It felt like an eternity. As if time had frozen me in that one moment that I so desperate sought to escape. It was the gentleman's voice that liberated me from that moment as it broke the silence.

"Please do forgive me madam," He said as he reached out to hand me my headdress. "I am terribly sorry, I didn't mean to remove this garment," He went on to explain, his hand still extended as I had yet to take the garment back. "Please... allow me to...," The gentleman was able to make out before I interjected causing his words to cease and resend.

"I guess you all can see now.... I know you have been wondering... well, now you know," I made out in a broken tone. "Though the freak show is over now... do enjoy your merry lives," I went on now balling hysterically.

Then I turned towards the door and made a run for it.

"Wait... just a moment madam," The gentleman called out as he made way after me.

"Just go away... please," I yelled back to him as I burst out of the door.

"Desire," a familiar voice call out that captured my attention.

I turned towards the voice while still running and noticed it was Rachel. The sight of her caused me to stop in my tracks. I wanted nothing more than for her to take me into her arms and comfort me.

"Madam look out," the Gentleman called out as he ran and dove towards me.

"Desire no," Rachel shouted in a panic.

Then I heard screeching of tires and massive horn. When I turned towards them, I was confronted with reality. My consciousness then transcended once more, and I found myself starring down at myself on life support. I looked so peaceful. Like I was submerged in a blissful sleep.

My consciousness then transcended once more. I now found myself starring down at the gentleman from the Boutique. He had flung himself in front of me in an attempt to save my life. My true knight in shinning armors. It was then I realized I did not even know my hero name. I looked at his arm bracelet and it read Benjamin Whip.

I then leaned over and gently kissed his lips and once more my consciousness was transcended. I now found myself with Rachel. She was painting. It was the night I told her about meeting Benjamin. Only this time, I realized that night for what it truly was.

Then I felt my consciousness transcend once more. I was now back at the fire. Benjamin eyes still piercing through. Only this time, we both knew. Not knowing at first seemed so much easier than knowing. Then there was a great peace I found in knowing. A peace that I marveled at.

As I lingered in that marvel Benjamins voice began to capture my attention.

"So, that is the truth of where we are my dear," Benjamin boldly proclaimed. Neither here nor there.... "Not dead... nor Alive," He went on.

Free to Fly

You never knew how much you wanted to live until you were fighting to survive...

You never understood why - except you were afraid to die...

But, when will you realize the real lies...

You... My love, shall never die...

For, the only thing that truly dies is matter...

That which you truly are not...

And the how or why, truly doesn't matter...

Just rest easy in the knowing my darling that you are now free to fly...

You are now free to fly...

So, go fly high above the mystic canyon...

Beyond the reach of this mortal dominion...
Abound far past the deep of the deepest opinions...

No need to beseech any mortal forgiveness...

For you are now free to fly...
Free to fly for all to witness...

Rest easy in knowing that you forwent the abyss...

& to it you returned to those you have missed...

In it you explore those things you have wished...

Where all things are possible...
Where all things are bliss...

A palace where you are now free to fly...
For you are now free to fly...

Free to Fly

LaVeL Regine

lavel.uk

www.ingramcontent.com/pod-product-compliance
Lightning Source LLC
Chambersburg PA
CBHW071959170626
46813CB00005B/1927